Pickles

Contents

Pioneer Valley Educational Press, Inc.

Chapter 1
The Smell

It was a beautiful sunny morning.
Pickles went outside.
Pickles loved being outside.

The birds in the trees were singing.
Pickles sat for a few minutes,
just listening to their songs.
Pickles was looking forward
to a long nap in a sunny spot
in the yard.

Suddenly, Pickles sat up.

She stopped listening to the birds.

Her tail went down, and her nose went up.

She sniffed the air.

What was that smell?

She sniffed again.

Pickles smelled something new in the yard!

Pickles walked around and sniffed.
Finally she found the spot
where the smell was coming from.
It was a huge hole!

Pickles looked and looked
at the hole.
The hole was huge!
Who made the huge hole?
The hole was not here yesterday!

Chapter 2
The Hole

Pickles walked around the hole.
She looked up and down
the yard. She got into the hole
and smelled it.
Pickles smelled and smelled the hole.
"A dog made this hole,"
thought Pickles. "I just know it."

Pickles was sure the hole was made by a dog. But what dog?
She sniffed again.

Pickles was mad.

"Strange dogs are not supposed to come into my yard and make big, huge holes!" thought Pickles.

Pickles worked and worked
to cover up the hole.
It was hard work for a little dog,
but soon the hole was gone.

Pickles went into the house to rest.

Mom looked at Pickles.
"Pickles, you are all dirty!
What have you been doing?
You are going to need a bath!"

"A bath? Oh, no!" thought Pickles.
She ran upstairs and hid
under Danny's bed.

Chapter 3
A Strange Dog

The next morning,
Pickles went outside.
It was another beautiful day,
but Pickles knew right away
that something was wrong.

She sniffed the air.
The smell was back!

Pickles ran across the yard.
The hole was back, and it was
bigger than ever!

Pickles was very mad.
She worked and worked to fill
the hole again.
Pickles got very dirty, so Mom
gave her another bath.
Pickles did *not* like baths!

After her bath, Pickles
went back outside.
She sat down in a spot
near the hole.

Pickles sat and watched
the hole. She watched and watched.
Who was making the hole?

Finally, a big, brown dog came
into the yard.

The dog went to the hole
and began digging.
The dog was much bigger
than Pickles, but Pickles
wasn't afraid. She was a brave dog.

"Woof, woof!" barked Pickles.
"Woof, woof!"

The big dog ignored Pickles
and kept on digging.

All of a sudden,
Pickles stopped barking.
She could see something
in the hole!

She could see *bones* in the hole!
Yes! There were lots
of yummy bones in the hole!

The strange dog picked up a bone
and ran off, leaving
the rest of them in the hole.

Oh, how Pickles loved bones!

Pickles jumped in the hole
with the bones.

Which one should she eat first?
There were big bones.
There were fat bones.
There were juicy bones.
It was so hard to decide!

"What a wonderful hole!"
thought Pickles.
"What wonderful, yummy bones!
And what a beautiful, sunny day!"